ZEEKA RETURNS

REVENGE OF ZEEKA BOOK 3

AUTHOR: BRENDA MOHAMMED

Contents

INTRODUCTION

Zeeka Returns provides some of the answers to your questions for the exciting five-part science fiction series, **Revenge of Zeeka.**

After days of searching for Zeeka and his zombies in the forest, the police could not find them.

Zeeka returned of his free will. He had a mission. Whether or not he accomplished that mission is for readers to find out.

What about his zombies?

It was the year 2036, and the island of Gosh had advanced in technology. At first, police tried the old method of using stakes.

It was not working well. Read how to kill zombies in a modern world.

If you have not read Book 1 and Book 2, you will find that the author has included parts of the previous two stories to guide you along.

MANHUNT ON FOR ZEEKA

After a very long and intensive interview with Dr. Steven Sharpe, the National Security Authorities on the island of Gosh launched a massive manhunt for Bill Grady, also known as Zeeka, and his nine flesh-eating zombies.

Law enforcement officers combed through densely forested areas on foot and all-terrain vehicles.
They believed that Grady and the zombies were hiding in those parts of the island.

The manhunt lasted for weeks and was the largest in the island's history. It involved numerous armed officers, armoured police vehicles, sniper teams, solar-powered helicopters, and tracker dogs.

The Government declared a National State of Emergency and warned nationals to keep their homes properly secured. Police raided Grady's home for information.

They discovered old newspaper clippings and several computer memory sticks with incriminatory information tying him to the kidnapping of seven-year-old Steven Sharpe almost forty years ago.

There was an undiscovered basement in Grady's house. Detective Jack Wildy and his assistant Jerry Cole found it and uncovered evidence that flesh-eating zombies lived there.

A smell of rotting meat filled the air. There were large chunks of beef and other types of meat in a deep freezer.

The Detectives found an unusually large locker, similar to the one that was at Steven's house. They could not open it as it required a code.
Police found makeshift campsites along the Orinoco River in the forest where

Zeeka and the zombies rested as they evaded the law.
Worst of all, there were many dead bodies strewn along the way.

It appeared that the zombies ripped out the hearts and livers of victims, leaving the carcasses in pools of blood.

"These killings could only have been the work of the zombies," said Detective Jack Wildy.

Jerry remarked, "If the zombies are unable to find victims, they may turn on Grady."

Jack did not agree with Jerry's statement and told him, "Remember he has the device to control them. He would not part with that device. He's smarter than that."

According to news reports, some police officers and other people suspected of assisting Grady with food supplies and equipment were arrested and interrogated, but Grady and the zombies remained at large.

Once again, the Island of Gosh was the subject of International Headlines in other parts of the world.

Manhunt on for rogue Chief of Police and nine zombies wanted for numerous vicious crimes in the island of Gosh.

Tourists cancelled all vacation plans to visit the island, and several countries published negative advisories to warn their nationals about travelling to Gosh.

The authorities in Gosh appointed a new Chief of Police named Bernard Stern. "Call me Bernie," he said to Jack Wildy and other senior members of his team.

Bernie was very pleasant and quite friendly, and although stockily built, he had a military look about him.
Quite unlike Bill Grady, he was a jolly fellow and a man of many words. He liked to chat about his days when he

served in the army in a foreign country. Sometimes Jack wished he would leave him to do his work.

Jack was sitting in his office at the station in deep thought. Numerous thoughts ran through his mind. He recalled the last words that Bill Grady said to him.

"Jack, I've something important to look after. I'm leaving for the day."

He wondered, *did Grady suspect that his criminal deeds would be exposed after our visit to the hideout. Did he leave that day to plan his escape? His office was clean when I had checked it. Did he deliberately clean out his office that day? Luckily for me, he forgot to take that flash drive with him, the one where he was speaking to Zombie number nine. How could he leave behind such incriminating evidence? Also, Raynor's brother, Steven, who was suspected of being Zeeka before the truth was uncovered, sent a flash drive with damaging information about him.*

Grady kidnapped him when he was just seven. All these years, and no one suspected Grady. He told Steven that he wanted to use the zombies in place of tracker dogs. This kidnapper and murderer was our Chief. How disgusting!

Jerry Cole walked in and saw Jack in a pensive mood. "Are you thinking about Bill Grady?"

Jack raised his head and replied, "I'm not going to rest until he's in custody. He has caused many deaths.
He must pay. I know the Government wants to call off the manhunt because it's too costly and impacts negatively on the national budget. However, I feel that we must find Grady and his zombies at any cost and restore the valuable reputation of this island. We cannot allow them to wreak havoc on this nation and escape justice. We need the assistance of Dr. Steven Sharpe."

“I agree with you. Steven Sharpe will know what to do to capture those zombies. He knows Grady’s secrets. Do you think he’s ready to help us, now that his name is cleared of all wrongdoing?”

“Maybe he will, or maybe he won’t. We have to try. Call Dr. Raynor Sharpe and ask him if he knows Steven’s whereabouts,” said Jack.

“I certainly will,” said Jerry.

STEVEN ASSISTS POLICE

At Raynor's home, there was happiness and laughter. Steven was enjoying a hearty breakfast with Raynor and Janet. Raynor and Steven were bringing each other up to date on their lives. Steven's biggest regret was not being able to grow up with his brother, Raynor.

He related his terrible experiences and nightmares after Grady kidnapped him at the age of seven. "He gave me everything I needed, but I was fearful of him. He threatened me on numerous occasions to kill our parents and you, Raynor, if I ever tried to run away. He was in the police force and had wide connections, so I had no choice but to stay with him."

"It's all in the past now, Steven. Detective Wildy got the District Attorney to clear you of any wrongdoing. You're free to live a normal life with your correct name, Steven Sharpe. No more living in fear for you. You will no longer be called Jason Stephens."

"It feels good to be called Steven Sharpe again. Let's drink to that," said Steven, as he raised his glass.

All three raised their glasses and carried on chatting merrily. Mark Schmidt arrived at that moment. Raynor warmly welcomed him to join them for breakfast. "Come in and sit down, Mark. We have enough food to feed an army."

The ringing of the visual phone interrupted them. The face of Jerry Cole appeared. "Good morning, Doc. How are you?"

Raynor replied, "Hi Jerry. I'm fine. We're having a brotherly reunion here."

Jerry was happy to hear Raynor's answer and asked, "Is your brother Steven with you?"

"Yes, he is," replied Raynor.

"I'm glad that you two reunited after so long. Can I speak to him?" asked Jerry. "What about?" asked Raynor. "I hope you are not all cooking up something against him."

Jerry laughed and said, "Oh no, Raynor. We need his help to find a way to stop those zombies. He's the only man who can do that because of his scientific expertise."

"I see. You need Steven's scientific help," said Raynor. "I'll put him on." Raynor called out to Steven and asked him to speak to Jerry. Steven obliged and went over to the phone and turned on the speaker. "Hi, Jerry. What's up?"

"Steven, I'm very sorry to bother you, but we desperately need your help. Those zombies are out of control, and Grady is not going to stop them. We need your expertise in this exercise.

Only you can devise something to end this massacre."

"I'll do anything to exterminate those zombies and put Grady behind bars. However, all the equipment was destroyed when Grady firebombed my house. It'll take a while to build a new device."

"Maybe Grady has some stuff at his house. When Jack Wildy and I searched that house, we found a locker that needs a code to open it. Would you happen to know that code?"

"Yes, I know the locker. I can open it. Can you pick me up? My electric car needs charging. I cannot use it."

"Sure, Wildy and I can be there within the next hour. Is that enough time for you?"

"That'll be fine. I'll finish up here with my brother and his wife and see you in an hour."

Steven turned the phone off and turned to Raynor, who said, “We heard it all Steven. Go help the police get rid of those killer zombies, and put Grady behind bars.”

Janet and Mark nodded in agreement and gave Steven the thumbs up.

FEARFUL CITIZENS PROTEST

Jack Wildy was very pleased when Jerry told him he had spoken to Steven Sharpe, and he had agreed to assist them. Jack said, “When this is all over, I am taking a month’s vacation and putting you in charge. You are showing me that you are a good assistant.”

“Thank you,” said Jerry. At that time a news flash came across the multimedia at the police station:

“Protestors are marching outside the President’s House protesting the mass killings, which continue along the Orinoco riverbed bearing placards such as these:
‘Islanders are living in fear. Stop the killings now.’
‘We fear for our lives. What are the police doing?’
‘Time for police to wake from their slumber and catch these criminals.’
‘We do not want to be eaten alive by Zombies. Do something now.’

'Is this government brain-dead? Bring down Zeeka and the Zombies.'

Jack, who was getting annoyed, said, "Turn that off, Jerry. Let's pick up Steven Sharpe. I want him to start working on something right away to blow away those zombies. I do not want to have to deal with an angry mob too. I want to see Grady chained and brought back to face justice. Let's go now."

Jack was angry after seeing the newsflash, and he did not hide his feelings. Jerry observed his mood.

"Allow me to drive," said Jerry, as he stretched his hand out to Jack for the car keys. Jack gave the keys willingly to Jerry as they walked out of the station.

They were both silent during the drive to pick up Steven Sharpe. Within a few minutes, they arrived at their destination. Steven was waiting in the driveway of Raynor's house for them.

When the car stopped, he opened the door to the back passenger seat and sat down. He acknowledged Jack and Jerry in a cheerful manner. “Good morning. How are you both?”

Jack responded, “Good morning to you. Shall we call you Steven or Doc?”

“Call me Steven,” he replied.

”Steven, we desperately need you to help us with this. Are you on board?” asked Jack.

“That’s why I am here, aren’t I? I want to see Grady pay for his misdeeds. Because of him, I lived a life without my parents and my only brother. It is my turn for revenge.”

Jerry turned around to look at Steven and said, “We’re on your side, Steven. In fact, we are all on the same side. And that is the side of the law.”

“Well said,” said Jack.

Soon they arrived at Grady's home. They came out of the car and walked up the path to the front door.
Turning to Steven, Jack asked, "Are you familiar with this house?"

Steven stood in front of the house and seemed a bit fearful for a moment. He then said, "Yes, it's where I grew up, or should I say, the place where I was imprisoned after being kidnapped. I hated this place. I hated Grady. Nevertheless, I stuck it out and survived, for one reason only. I did not want him to carry out his threats to hurt my family if I tried to leave him."

"And you could not report him to the police because he was a cop," said Jerry.

Jack shook his head and could only say, "Sad, very sad," as they entered the house.

"We should get to that locker in the basement right away," said Jerry leading the way.
Steven and Jack followed him. The stench in the basement was more pungent than it had been a few days before, and they had to cover their noses with masks, which Jerry had brought along with him.
Steven went to the unusually large locker and clapped three times. There was a click, and the door slid open.

"Wow," said Jerry.
"We never guessed it was that easy."

Jack remarked, "How impressive. Let's see what's in here."
"What's this?" shouted Jack. "Are these stakes to kill zombies the old fashioned way? There are nine of them." Turning his attention to the other items in the locker he shouted, "Look at these! They're the latest model in high-powered weapons. These rifles can kill from a mile off and set off a trail of fire. He must have taken them from the

station." Jack held up a demolisher 549 to show Steven and Jerry.
"Steven interjected, "What I need to do is build a reverse transponder that will modify the actions in the false heads of those zombies. Once you have that, you can slow them down, gather them in one place, and the police can use the stakes and weapons to kill them."

"You make it sound easy," said Jack.

"It's not easy," said Steven. "To build that transponder, I must have a false head from one of the zombies."

Jack was quick to answer, "We have one at the station. It had belonged to Zombie Nine. He threw it out on the stage before the attack at the Carnival Celebrations in February."

"Oh yes. I heard about that. Well let's get it, and I can start work on the transponder," said Steven gleefully.

“Steven, how long will it take you to build that transponder?” Jack asked. “It can be ready in the morning if I get that false head today,” Steven replied.

“All right, Steven. I will get it for you on my return to the station. Jerry and I will discuss with the Chief and have a team ready to go into the forest tomorrow. Are you going with us to the woods? We’ll do our best to ensure your safety,” said Jack to Steven.

Jerry said, “Steven’s a civilian. It’s against the rules. We cannot take him into the forest with us. Once he builds the transponder, I’ll operate it.”

“You’re right, Jerry. I was joking. I know how much Steven wants us to bring in Grady,” said Jack.

Steven replied, “Best of luck guys. Dr. Brown offered me my old job at the Central Hospital. I start there tomorrow.”

"Congratulations,” said Jack.

“I’m very pleased for you,” said Jerry. Turning to Jerry, Jack said, “Call one of the officers on duty to come with a vehicle to move this stuff to the station.”

RAYNOR HIRES A HELPER

Steven returned to Raynor's home, and a beautiful female face greeted him. She was alluring. He was taken aback. "Am I in the right house?" he asked.

The person replied in a voice that sounded like a recording. "You're at the home of Dr. Raynor Sharpe. May I help you?"

It dawned on Steven that a robot was speaking to him. She was very humanlike. Her eyes were like a camera, and she spoke fluently. She was extremely attractive and looked like a real woman. He was staring at her in amazement when he heard a chuckle.

Raynor emerged from the kitchen, and in a laughing voice, he said, "This is our new helper. She's here on a trial basis. If she works out, we'll keep her. If not, Janet's older sister, Mandy, would come to stay with us until Janet has the baby."

“I’ll be a good helper, sir,” the robot said.

“What is your name?” asked Steven.

“My name is Miranda. I am here to serve you.”

Steven looked at her admiringly. “Thank you, Miranda. You can go to the kitchen now. Janet needs you,” said Raynor.

“Times have certainly changed,” said Steven, as both he and Raynor watched Miranda saunter off to the kitchen.

“She’s a taekwondo expert too. She’ll be proper protection for Janet, and of course, all of us,” said Raynor.

“She looks amazing,” said Steven. ”She’ll be very useful.”

The doorbell rang, and someone shouted out, “Package for Dr. Steven Sharpe.”

Raynor ran downstairs to get it. He collected it and handed it to Steven. "What's that?" he asked Steven.

"It's a false head of one of the zombies. I have to build a reverse transponder to modify the actions of the zombies who're on the run."

"Was that the head of Zombie number nine?" asked Raynor.

"Yes, it is. Wildy said so. He kept it at the station after he found it," said Steven.

"Do you have the necessary elements and tools to do that?"

"Yes, I stopped off at the technology shop and got the stuff I needed. I am going to the garage to work on this right away. Jack Wildy and Jerry Cole need the transponder in the morning. They are going into the forest with a team to hunt those zombies down and to bring in Grady."

“I know you’ll be able to do this. I’m sorry, I cannot be of any help on the scientific side of things. I’m rushing off to the hospital now. I have patients waiting. See you later.”

Steven waved to Raynor and said, “Bye, Raynor.”

After Raynor left, Steven went into the garage and started working immediately on the new transponder.

The following morning, Jack and Jerry arrived to collect it. Stephen spent a full hour explaining to the two detectives how to use it. After thanking Steven, Jack and Jerry went off to meet a team to go to the forest to track down Grady and the zombies. The team took along the stakes and other weapons, which they found in the locker in the basement of Grady’s home.

“It’s going to be a rough day,” said Jack to Jerry.

“I’m well-prepared, mentally,” said Jerry.

"Are you scared to face those zombies?" Jack asked Jerry.

"I never had an encounter with zombies before. I must admit that I'm having chills up my spine," replied Jerry.

"You're not alone. You are certainly not alone. It's a first for everyone on the team," said Jack.

HAMMER ESCAPES DEATH

Before leaving the station, the Chief of Police had gathered his men and planned a strategy for the proposed attack. He warned them, however, that Grady was a former Chief of Police and would be planning a counterattack to avert capture.

He assigned the Deputy Chief, George Hammer, to lead the officers, and Jack and Jerry agreed to join them. As they drove through the heavily forested area in all-terrain vehicles, some officers held on to the stakes and weapons, in preparation for the ambush.

Other officers had stun grenades within close reach.
Jack and Jerry, who were in a separate vehicle with two officers, had the reverse transponder ready; to freeze the action of the zombies should they attack.

The forest appeared calm with no sign of life anywhere. Jack spoke to the officers in the vehicle behind him on the car mobile, "The sound of the police helicopters in the air may have alerted Grady. They're probably hiding out in an area where no one can spot them. Fire off some shots to get them active."

No sooner had Jack said those words, a few shots rang out in the air.

Deputy Hammer made a suggestion. "I believe that we should park the vehicles now and walk through the forest on foot. Grady will not allow all nine zombies to assemble in one place. He will send them out one by one. We can lay low in this section." He pointed to a grassy area by a stone wall, which was not clearly visible to anyone traversing that area.

"You're right," said Jack, picking up the car mobile, "I'll contact the others now." They stepped out of their vehicles and formed a human barricade around the area, making sure to keep out of sight. They were there for a few minutes when one zombie showed his face.

The zombie was enormous and scary-looking, with blood dripping from his mouth. It looked as if he had just eaten an animal. He was wielding a hatchet. Jerry tried to reverse the "attack mode" in his false head with the new transponder that Steven had made. He fumbled a few times with the instrument and finally got it to work. The zombie stood frozen in one position, and Officer Larry Swan bravely ran up to him and drove a stake through his body. He fell to the ground. Another officer fired shots at him with a demolisher 549, and the zombie was consumed in fire.

"How gross!" one officer said. Another said, "Let them come and face the same fate as that first one. One bloody zombie met his downfall. Now there are eight more bloody zombies to kill."

“That was terrifying. How long do we have to wait for the others to appear?” asked Jerry.

“Grady has lost one of his zombies. He’ll put up a serious fight now. He might wait until we’re exhausted before he sends another zombie after us. We have to remain alert, or he’ll attack us unawares,” Jack replied.

“You’re right, Jack,” Hammer said. ”Our men should make use of the power snacks now. I think that they can last a few more hours on the supplies that we have. It seems that this operation may take us a very long time. Grady will stretch this out. I’m going to call him out on the microphone and see what he does.”

Deputy Chief Hammer took out the microphone equipment from one of the vehicles and announced, “Grady, wherever you are, we have you surrounded. You cannot escape even with those zombies as your protection.

Come out with your hands up and direct those zombies to do the same."

There was still no movement, and the officers waited in silence for almost an hour as they munched on snacks. Hammer repeated the call several times, but to no avail. He then turned to the team and said, "Looks like we'll have to call it a day. Pack up boys. We'll have to come back tomorrow and go deeper into the forest. It seems that Grady and the remaining zombies have retreated further."

"Are you sure we should leave now?" asked Jerry.

"I agree with Hammer, boy. Let's pack up," said Jack.

In the blink of an eye, an axe hurtled through the air and almost grazed Hammer's face. One inch closer and it would have taken off his neck. The axe landed at Hammer's feet, and he stood frozen to the ground.

"Look out!" screamed Jerry, as a zombie came in full view of everyone with his killer gadgets turned on in his false head. Jerry immediately turned on the transponder in his hand to reverse the zombie's actions, and the zombie halted.

"Drive the stake in," Hammer shouted to the officers. Officer Swan ran up to the zombie and drove a stake into him. Hammer grabbed a demolisher 549 and fired on the zombie, reducing him to ashes.

Hammer, who was obviously shaken after a close encounter with death, turned to them and said, "Guys, I know that you all need to rest. Let's leave this place now. We'll return tomorrow refreshed to finish off this job."

They obeyed without argument.

OFFICER SWAN HURT

The following day Deputy Chief Hammer took his team deeper into the forest, and for a very long while, they could see no signs of Grady and the seven zombies. Eventually, they parked the vehicles near a shady area on the banks of the river, as it was impossible to drive any further. Blood and bones of dead animals were scattered everywhere. It was evident that the zombies were nearby.

Hammer spoke to his men. “We’d have to make it on foot from here on. Offload all the equipment and set up a tent. Officer Swan, we now have exactly seven stakes. I’m entrusting you with the job of driving those stakes into the remaining seven zombies if there’s a need to do so. Jerry, you have the most important part to play with that transponder. You’ve done a great job so far, and I’m relying on you to neutralize those zombies so that Officer Swan can use the stakes. The rest of the team can use the demolisher rifles to finish them off as necessary. Use the stun grenades only if we have a real battle on our hands. We want the zombies dead, but we want Grady alive. I know after yesterday's stakeout, you all are exhausted and even frustrated. This operation is not an easy one. However, to survive, we must remain alert. Any questions?"

The men all indicated non-verbally they had no issues and proceeded to offload the ammunition.

Hours passed, and there were no signs that Grady and the zombies were around. The officers were becoming restless when they suddenly heard a rustling sound in the bushes.

Two zombies were heading towards them. One of them surprised Officer Swan, who had his back turned to them and threw a hatchet at him. The hatchet almost severed his right arm, and he bled profusely.

Hammer dragged Swan to safety and tried to stop the bleeding. The other zombie raised his hatchet to attack another officer, but he threw a stake at him in time. The stake caught the zombie's leg; the hatchet fell, and the zombie started hopping around on one foot as if he were doing a zombie dance.

All this time Jerry was trying to destabilize the zombies with the transponder, but it fell from his hands. In a mad rush to protect themselves, two officers grabbed two more stakes, ran up to the zombies, and pierced them through their hearts. Another used the demolisher 549 and fired at them. Their bodies disintegrated, and the officers breathed a sigh of relief.

Four zombies were down, and there were five more to go.

There was no time to waste. Officer Swan had lost lots of blood, needed urgent medical treatment, and had to be rushed to the hospital. Hammer and three officers took him in one of the vehicles and sped off to the Central Hospital.

The other men packed up the equipment and left the forest for the day with sombre faces. It was a horrifying experience for all. Four zombies were down, but the officers were not happy. Their colleague, Officer Swan, had been severely injured.

Dr. George Brown was speaking to a patient in the emergency ward, and he saw when they brought in Officer Swan. He immediately arranged with the surgeons and nurses on duty, to perform surgery to repair Swan's arm.

Hammer related to Brown what had taken place in the forest. Brown was visibly upset when he heard the details.

Nurse Giselle ran to Swan's side in tears and shouted, "No, Larry. How could this happen to you?"

Hammer asked Dr. Brown, "Do you know that Larry Swan is Giselle's husband?"

George Brown shook his head and replied, "Yes, I met him once." He reached out to console Giselle.

News about the zombie attack on Swan quickly spread around the hospital. Raynor, Janet, Mark, and other doctors and nurses rushed to Nurse Giselle's side to comfort her. Chief of Police Joseph Stern sped over to the hospital to see Swan.

News reporters and television crews crowded the hospital grounds to get interviews from officers who were present at the stakeout.

SWAN DIES

The next day Hammer and his team ventured into the forest with strong feelings of bitterness. After what transpired the day before, they were forced to wear heavy vests and camouflage suits in the blazing tropical heat for added protection.

Hammer reflected on his narrow escape with death two days before when the zombie's axe flew in his direction.

Then the following day another zombie threw a hatchet at Officer Swan almost severing his right arm. It was their third day in their search for Grady also known as Zeeka, and his nine zombies. His thoughts were all about capturing Grady and getting rid of the remaining five zombies.

Hammer knew that his bosses wanted Grady alive to answer several serious charges of murder and kidnapping.

He muttered under his breath, *"If I could just throw a few hand grenades in their path it would be very easy. However, I must do this the right way if we are to keep Grady alive. Besides, hand grenades will cause a bushfire."*

His phone rang at that moment. Dr. Brown's face appeared, and Hammer turned on the speaker as Brown spoke. "Hammer, I have bad news. Swan just succumbed to his injury. The hatchet was poisonous. The poison consumed his body before we even prepared him for surgery to re-attach his arm."

"What?" Hammer shouted. "The hatchet was poisonous? Grady must pay for this and much more. Swan did not deserve to die like that. He was one of my best men." Tears welled up in his eyes.

"Be careful out there," Dr. Brown replied. "Those zombies are extremely dangerous."

Hammer, who was overcome with grief, answered, "We will be careful. How is Nurse Giselle doing? She must be heartbroken to lose her husband like that. Please convey my sympathies to her.

Dr. Brown replied, "She is not doing well at all, but we are doing our best to comfort her. Will see you all later."

As Hammer turned off his phone, he turned to his officers who had heard the entire conversation and said, "Let's hunt them down. Let's find these killers now."

His men felt motivated by the same anger and vengeance that Hammer felt after hearing that Swan had died. They shouted in unison, "We will attack with full force, sir."

Hammer commanded, “Get those grenades out. We will make Grady pay.” It seemed that Hammer and his men had lost all reasoning. They wanted revenge for the death of their partner. Their mission was to kill even it meant disobeying orders and killing Grady too.

They were unaware that Grady was eavesdropping in some nearby bushes. Upon hearing the determination of the officers to kill him, he abandoned the five zombies and hurried out of the forest.

What was on Grady’s mind? Where was he heading? Would he be safer where he was going?

MIRANDA CAPTURES ZEEKA

Grady was out of breath as he ran, walked, and jumped over many obstacles on his way out of the forest. He knew that no one would be looking for him in the civilized parts of the island.

Hammer and his team were searching for him in the forest. They would be there a long time. It no longer mattered to him if they found and killed the zombies. He no longer needed them. He needed to do something important, and he wanted to stay alive to do that.
His only weapon was a gun, but he did not intend to use that, at least not yet. He was on a mission, maybe an impossible one. Nevertheless, he was going to try. As he approached the main road, he covered his head with a hood to hide his identity.

Cars zoomed past him, and fortunately, no one recognized him.

He was shabbily dressed and looked like a homeless person, having lived in the forest for many days. He hoped that some people would mistake him for a hunter, except he had no game to show for it.

He crossed the main road at the intersection and made his way towards the beach, trying to keep out of sight as much as he could. He passed several houses and then stopped at a magnificent home overlooking the beach. He hesitated a while and then walked into the driveway.

He walked up the steps to the front door, gun in hand, and knocked on the door. For a while, there was no answer. Then the door opened, and a beautiful smiling young woman peeped out. On seeing the gun in his hand, her smile turned to a frown.

Grady was stunned to see such a beautiful woman and asked, “Do you live here?”

She stared at him as she scrutinized him before answering, "Yes, I live here. What are you doing here with a weapon?"

Realizing that the gun was upsetting her, Grady placed it against the wall and said, "I'm not here to harm anyone. I only want to see Steven Sharpe. I have something important to tell him."

Her eyes flashed, and it was apparent that she was enraged. "You come here with a gun to tell Dr. Sharpe something important? I do not believe you." She swung around, lifted one foot in the air, and kicked him down the stairs.

Grady was shocked and in severe pain. He tried to get up but could not. He was sure that he had broken several bones. She looked at him from the top of the stairs and said menacingly, "You cannot fool Miranda. I sense that your intentions are evil."

Groaning at the bottom of the stairs, Grady said to her, “You are a robot, aren’t you?”

Miranda did not answer Grady. She stomped down the stairs and grabbed him while he yelled out in pain. From out of nowhere, a tie-wrap appeared, and she swiftly used it to secure Grady’s arms behind his back.
Then he heard her say, “There is a man with a gun at the home of Dr. Raynor Sharpe. Come immediately.”

Grady knew right away that the robot had activated her built-in security system, which she used to apprehend him and contact the police.
He was in too much pain to get up and run. There was no escape for him.

Within minutes, the Chief of Police, Bernard Stern, and a couple of officers arrived at the house and found Grady, tied and bound, lying at the bottom of the stairs.

They congratulated Miranda, arrested him, and took him to prison. Stern contacted Hammer and told them that Grady was in custody. They were shocked to hear that Miranda, a robot, was responsible for his capture.

They were surprised to hear what the Chief had to say about the tactics she used.

They immediately returned to the station. However, Hammer and his men were puzzled as to why Grady left the forest without the zombies.

A few minutes afterward, Raynor, Janet, and Steven returned home. Miranda had sent them text messages about what happened.

"You handled yourself well," said Raynor to Miranda. "You caught the most wanted criminal on the island. You did something that the police have been trying to do for weeks."

Miranda smiled and said, "Thank you, sir."
Steven asked, "You said that he wanted to tell me something important, but he brought along a gun?"

Miranda shook her head. "Yes, sir. That is why I used my taekwondo skills to disable him. I thought he came to kill you, and I could not let him do that."

Janet was very pleased to hear Miranda say that. She said, "Miranda, you're amazing. We're keeping you. Do you agree on this, Raynor?"

Raynor was smiling. He turned to Miranda and said, "Of course, I do. Miranda, from today you are no longer working on a trial basis. We're employing you permanently. I am going to call the recruitment company right away to confirm."

That night, Raynor's home was flooded with phone calls from news media. They had many visitors, among them Jack

Wildy and Jerry Cole. They heaped praises on Miranda for capturing Grady.

ZEEKA CONFESSES

Bill Grady had a lot to answer for. He was in chains and sat in the interrogation room.

Chief of Police Bernard Stern, Jack Wildy, Jerry Cole, and Deputy Chief George Hammer walked in. Grady, the former Chief of Police, suddenly felt embarrassed to be on the other side of the law. He hung his head in shame. Stern spoke first. “Hammer read Grady his rights.”

Hammer read from a device, “Bill Grady, you have the right to remain silent. Anything you say may be used against you in a court of law.” Grady shook his head and remained silent.

Stern then said, “Grady, it hurts me to know that you were in charge of law and order on the island of Gosh. Today you are facing multiple criminal charges. You have one phone call to contact an attorney before we read out those charges to you. Do you want to call an attorney?"

Grady was all bruised and battered from the encounter with Miranda. He looked dejected. "Can I see the charges you have listed in that tablet in your hands?" he asked.

"This is only an outline of the two hundred-plus charges against you. A detailed official document is being prepared. But you can have a look at this," said Stern as he passed the tablet to Grady.

Grady read aloud the list of charges dated 25th June 2036. His voice was muffled.

The kidnapping of seven-year-old Steven Sharpe, son of Dr. Carl Sharpe [deceased] and Margaret Sharpe [deceased], in 1996.

Illegally removing 60 dead babies from the Central hospital in 2016 and creating zombies with their bodies.

Instigating 51 zombies to massacre a crowd of people at the National Carnival celebrations in February 2036. In that massacre, 125 people died, and 75 were maimed for life. [200 charges].

Harbouring nine flesh-eating zombies at a basement in a private home, for the sole purpose of doing grievous bodily harm to residents of Gosh.

The murder of Officer Larry Swan on 24th June 2036.

The murder of several victims in the forested area by zombies controlled by you. [full list being compiled]

Home invasion and attempted murder at the home of Dr. Raynor Sharpe on 24th June 2036.

After reading through the list, Grady said, "I do not need a lawyer. I will sign a confession to everything. I can run no more. First, I want to see Steven Sharpe. I have something important to tell him. That's the reason I went yesterday, to the house where he is staying. I did not intend to harm anyone.

Please, can you grant me this one wish?"

Stern replied, "I'll call Steven, but it's up to him. I'm not sure that he wants to speak to you. We have some questions for you. Where are the five remaining zombies? In what part of the forest can they be found?"

"I will draw a map for you. Can I have a pen and paper, please?" Grady asked. One of the officers handed him a pen and paper. Grady willingly drew the map and gave it to Stern.

Stern then gave the map to Hammer and said to Grady, "Where is the transponder to control the zombies?" Grady looked as if he was trying to retrace his movements. "I left the bag with it in the forest."

"That'll be all, for now, Grady. The officers will take you back to your cell. I'll contact Steven for you," said Stern.

Two prison officers escorted Grady back to his cell.

Jack turned to the others and said, “So a robot captured the most wanted criminal in Gosh. Isn’t that something?”

Hammer replied, “Yeah. That’s a first. Grady must have overheard us talking in the forest, abandoned his zombies, and sneaked up to Raynor’s house, where Steven is staying.”

Jerry Cole said, “We need some robots with taekwondo skills in the police force. Miranda destabilized him with one spin kick.”

Jack did a quick search on his tablet. “I think it is called a ‘jump reverse kick.' Jerry, we should go for taekwondo training. It seems like we’ll need it.”

Stern interjected. “On a more serious note, we have to assist Giselle to prepare for Larry’s funeral. I want him to have a dignified funeral.

He was a brave police officer killed in the line of duty for his country. Hammer, you and your men must find those zombies and destroy them. I'll call Steven about Grady's request."

When the men left the prison, news reporters and television camera personnel were waiting outside for interviews.
Gosh was the subject of international headlines again. Headlines in newspapers, social media, and television all over the world read, 'Zeeka Returns.'

ZEEKA COMMITS SUICIDE

Bernard Stern called Steven Sharpe to advise him of Grady's request. Steven reluctantly agreed when Stern assured him that he would personally see to it that the prison officers protected him. He went to the jail, and two prison officers brought Grady to the front to speak with him.

The officers chained Grady heavily to a chair and stood up close to him. Steven asked, "About what do you want to see me? Have you not done enough harm in my life? Why did you come to Raynor's house yesterday and scare Miranda with a gun? Do you want to kill me now?"

Grady replied, "No Steven, I do not want to kill you. I only want to apologise to you and to tell you why I kidnapped you forty years ago."

Steven snapped, “You are forty years too late. What can you say to me now that I do not know already?”

Grady went on, “Steven, I thought you were my son.”

Steven laughed sarcastically. “Ha! What on earth made you think that?” asked Steven.

“Your mother and I were engaged to be married,” Grady said.

Steven got up to leave and said, “I do not believe that. You are trying to manipulate me once again.”

Grady pleaded with Steven. “Steven, please sit down. I am speaking the truth. Your mother and I were in love. We got engaged without her father’s permission, and he did everything in his power to prevent our marriage.”

Steven sat down, and Grady continued. “The good doctor did not want his daughter to marry a police officer. He wanted her to marry your father, who was also a physician. She listened to her father, and she jilted me. I could not get over her. I thought that you were my son. I asked her, and she denied it, and I did not believe her."

Steven got up again to leave. "You are a sick man, Grady. You thought I was your son, so you kidnapped me?"

Grady tried his best to convince Steven to stay and listen to him. "I have loved you as if you were my own. I sent you to medical school so you would become famous just like your biological father. Everything I have belongs to you. I made a will. My attorney will contact you after I am gone," said Grady.

"I do not want anything that belongs to you. After you are gone, you say. You are not going anywhere except behind bars for the rest of your life. You robbed me of my life with my parents and only brother. You forced me to make a vaccine so you could create those zombies. You told me you wanted to introduce them into the police force as robots instead of tracker dogs. But what did you do? You used them to kill and maim people for your personal vendetta. I cannot listen to any more of this." Steven was ready to leave once more.

Grady held on to him, pleading, "I beg of you. Before you leave, please forgive me. I need your forgiveness. Steven, I'm sorry."

Steven pulled his hand away and signaled to the officers to open for him and without replying to Grady, he walked out. The two officers returned Grady to his cell.

A young prison officer, Brian Stoute, stood guard outside the cell. Grady called out to him, "Can you bring me some water, please? I'm not feeling well."
Stoute knew that Grady was the former Chief of Police and still had some

respect for him. He immediately left his post and went to a nearby cooler to get it. He returned with a plastic glass of water, opened the cell, and went up to Grady with it.

Grady took the glass, had a sip, dashed it to the ground, wrapped his arm around the neck of the officer, and grabbed his gun. He then threw the officer aside and shot himself in the head. Other prison officers rushed to the scene on hearing the gunshot. Grady was already dead.

When Steven returned to Raynor's home, news reporters and television personnel were interviewing Miranda for her heroic actions in having Grady captured. One reporter approached him to tell his story about how Grady kidnapped him when he was just seven years old, and he willingly did so. His conversation with Grady a few minutes before assisted him with what he had to say.

Later that evening, Steven lay on his bed thinking about his conversation with Grady. What did he mean by '*after I am gone*'? Where was he going? Why was he begging for forgiveness? The phone rang. Someone in the house answered it.

A few minutes afterward, there was a knock on Steven's door. He opened it and saw Raynor standing there looking stunned. "What's the matter, bro?" Steven asked Raynor.

"Bernard Stern just called. He said that Grady feigned an illness and asked for water. When the prison officer went to give him the water, he overpowered him, took his gun away, and shot himself. He's dead."

Steven was speechless. He understood what Grady meant by '*after I am gone*.' The two brothers hugged each other in silence for one minute, and then Raynor said, "It's over. You can now get on with your life."

ZOMBIES DEMOLISHED

The news of Grady's death spread across the island and internationally. Nationals rejoiced. Some shouted in the streets, "Zeeka is dead!" However, some people came out with placards demanding that the police find the remaining five zombies and destroy them.

Hammer and his men returned the next day to complete their mission in the forest to hunt and kill the zombies. Jack and Jerry stayed at the station to tie up loose ends on the capture and suicide of Bill Grady. Jerry gave the reverse transponder to Hammer.

Armed with all the necessary weapons, they trudged through the narrow trails keeping alert in their quest for the zombies. Hammer had a lot on his mind. His thoughts were on Larry Swan who had died the day before, and on his former chief, Grady who was also

known as Zeeka, and who killed himself at the prison.
He was thinking, "*The things Grady did are bizarre. He must have had a warped mind. I had much respect for him, and we are now in this situation because of him. Swan died at the hands of one of those zombies because of Grady. Our lives are in danger because of him and those zombies. I hope he rots in Hell*."

The map, which Grady had drawn for them, had proven to be useful. They found the lair of the zombies with ease. However, the zombies were nowhere in sight. Grady's bag was lying in the large enclosed tent, and upon opening it, they discovered the transponder required to control the zombies.

Hammer immediately turned off "Attack Mode." He did that to ensure the safety of the officers or anyone walking through the forest. He checked the bag again and what he found was unbelievable. It was a Szalinzki's Shrinking Machine.

"Holy cow!" he exclaimed. "Did Grady have plans to get rid of these zombies himself by shrinking them."

"Sir," shouted Officer Cameron. "I can see them. They're under that tree down that hill."

Hammer looked down the hill. He spotted the zombies. They seemed lost without their Master. "Good for them," said Hammer. "Look what I found. Grady had the latest technology in his bag. It is Szalinzki's Shrinking Machine to shrink the zombies. It seems that he was planning to kill them himself."

"Is that a shrinkenator? Do you know how to use it?" asked Cameron.

Hammer looked over the machine and said, "That's a good question. Do you?"

Cameron stretched out his hand. "Can I see it?"

Hammer held up his hands and covered his face. “Be careful now, Cameron. Don’t point that thing at any of us.”

The other officers gathered around to see the machine. “I’ll be careful,” Cameron replied, as he examined it carefully. “There is a lever in the middle. If I move this forward like this, it may work.” As he spoke, he turned around, pointed the machine in the direction of the zombies and moved the lever.

The zombies squealed loudly and shrank in size to mere midgets. They became easy targets after that, as the officers threw stun grenades at them and reduced them to ashes with the demolishers 549. There was no need for stakes. “It worked. It worked,” shouted Officer Cameron.

“Mission accomplished,” said Hammer. “Good job Cameron. Good job officers. The Chief will be proud of us. I filmed the entire episode with the camera in my hat. I’ll show the video to the Chief, and we can give it to the media to publish. There'll be no more protests from nationals. Let's leave this place and return to civilisation."

FUNERAL OF OFFICER SWAN

Chief of Police Bernard Stern was very proud of his men. They had destroyed nine dangerous zombies. He prepared to hold a press conference after Larry Swan's funeral the following day. He had plans to make honorable mention of some of his men, and others for bravery, and had invited the relevant parties to attend.

However, the funeral of Larry Swan was uppermost in his mind as he entered the Gosh Presbyterian church wearing a grey flannel suit. Numerous officers and other people who knew Officer Larry and Nurse Giselle filled the pews. The coffin with Larry's body was lying in front of the altar, and his wife was sitting in the front seat just behind it.

She was weeping uncontrollably, and her relatives were comforting her. The police officers were all dressed in black long sleeved shirts and black pants.

Shiny medals sparkled on the shirts of some officers. Stern became emotional when he saw the coffin and packed church. He stood frozen at the entrance.

An usher came up to him and led him to a section at the front, reserved for Giselle's and Larry's closest colleagues. Dr. Raynor Sharpe, his wife Dr. Janet Jones – Sharpe, Dr. Steven Sharpe, and Miranda the robot arrived soon after. The usher led them to the reserved seats. Next to arrive, were Dr. George Brown and Dr. Mark Schmidt. Jack Wildy and Jerry Cole turned up after a few minutes followed by Deputy Chief George Hammer and Officer Cameron. Before taking their seats, they greeted Giselle and offered their condolences.

The funeral service started promptly at 3.00 pm and ended at 4.00 pm. Cremation of his body took place at a nearby funeral home one hour later. After the cremation, Giselle asked the hospital doctors, Police Chief, and

others who were close to Larry to partake of a meal at her home.
Chief of Police Bernard Stern walked around and talked to everyone present. The people of Gosh found him warm, friendly, and a man of action. He walked up to Raynor and Janet, who was wearing a black maternity dress and remarked, "Congratulations. I see that both of you are going to be parents soon."
They were surprised that he noticed Janet's pregnancy.

"Oh yes, we are very grateful parents-to-be," Raynor answered.

"Your helper Miranda is a heroic robot. You both are lucky to have her. We need more robots like her in homes, and maybe in the police force. She courageously cornered the most wanted criminal on this island. I am going to give her honorable mention in my press conference tomorrow. Oh, there is Steven. I need to talk to him. Have a good night. By the way, call me Bernie," said Stern to Raynor and Janet.

"What a warm and candid person he is," said Janet.

Stern walked up to Steven, put his arm around his shoulders, and led him out to the verandah. He turned to him and said, "Steven, I know that Grady spoke to you just before he committed suicide. I feel sorry for him. Someone has to bury him. You were all he had.
I know he kidnapped you when you were just seven years old, and you feel a strong resentment towards him. Would you..........?"

Steven raised his hand and stopped Stern from continuing. "Would I arrange for his burial? I have been thinking about it. He begged me to forgive him. I will do it, but it will be a small private funeral. I would want you and George Hammer there."

Stern was pleased with Steven's positive response. "Certainly. I will attend. I will tell Hammer. What day do you have in mind?" he asked.

"I was thinking about tomorrow. I still have to tell Raynor and Janet about it," Steven replied.

"That's settled then, Steven. My press conference is tomorrow morning, so can you have it in the afternoon, say 3.00 pm? You lifted a burden off my shoulder. After all, he was the former Chief of police."

Steven shook his head in agreement and went off to tell Raynor and Janet.

PRESS CONFERENCE

The following day at the press conference Bernard Stern made the following speech:
"Members of the media, the national community, and all those present here, I am proud to inform you today, 27th June 2036, that the terror which surrounded the island of Gosh over the past few weeks is over. My men have worked extremely hard to bring closure to this matter.
Bill Grady, also known as Master Zeeka, was apprehended at the home of Raynor and Janet Sharpe when he went with a gun to look for Steven Sharpe who now resides there.
Miranda, the robot, was home alone at the time. She did not know who he was, but when she saw the gun in his hand, she sensed that he was not a friend. She used her taekwondo skills to impair him and activated her built-in security system to contact the police. I applaud Miranda for her bravery.

Deputy Chief Hammer and his team combed the forest for many days where Grady and the zombies were hiding out, and they successfully destroyed all nine zombies.
Officer Larry Swan, now deceased, and Officer Cameron played significant roles in the destruction of those zombies.
By now, you would have heard that Grady has committed suicide.
He feigned illness, asked for water, overpowered the brave guard, Brian Stoute, who went to give it to him, grabbed his gun, and shot himself.
He was your former Chief of police. He was the one appointed to one of the highest positions in this island to protect and serve you and your families. Sad to say, he let you all down.
It hurts me. Ladies and gentlemen, to remind you of the massacre which he instigated at the annual Carnival Celebrations in February this year.
One hundred and twenty- five persons were killed, and seventy-five maimed for life when he used a scientific experiment to take revenge for a personal

grievance, which he harboured for twenty years.
He used fifty-one zombies that he claimed he wanted to use in place of tracker dogs in that attack.
One zombie removed his false head and threw it some distance away.
It appeared that the zombie did not want to kill anyone.
His fake head proved to be a valuable clue in solving the case.
That is not the end of it.
Grady kept nine flesh-eating zombies in the basement of his home for sinister purposes.
You have seen on television and read in the electronic news of the bloody killings for which these zombies were responsible.
Bill Grady had more than 200 charges against him. He even kidnapped a seven-year-old boy forty years ago.
That boy is alive today and has told his story many times. He is Dr. Steven Sharpe.
Grady had changed the boy's name to Jason Stephens and threatened to kill

his parents and brother if he ever told anyone that he had kidnapped him.

The boy could not report him to the police because Grady was a high-ranking rogue officer who knew how to twist the truth to suit himself.
The District Attorney has absolved Dr. Steven Sharpe of any blame in the murders perpetrated by Grady.
I must commend Dr. George Brown, Dr. Raynor Sharpe, and Dr. Mark Schmidt for first bringing the matter of Zeeka and the Zombies to the police's attention.

Detectives Jack Wildy and Jerry Cole took the matter seriously and worked with the doctors to discover the truth in this issue, and I commend them for their hard work and determination.

I want to assure the public that as your new Chief of Police, I am here to protect and to serve. Never again must this island experience anything like Zeeka and the Zombies.

My deputy and I are now available for questions."
The media did not miss an opportunity to ask questions, and the next day, Stern's speech and answers to follow-up questions flooded the world news.

Later in the day, Steven Sharpe, Raynor, Janet Sharpe, Bernard Stern, Dr. George Brown, Dr. Mark Schmidt, and George Hammer gathered at a small funeral home for a private cremation of Bill Grady.

After the priest had performed the last rites and his body committed, Grady's attorney, Tom Saunders, walked in and handed a letter to Steven.
Steven opened the letter. It contained a cheque for a substantial amount and the deed to several properties owned by Grady.

Steven announced, "I am making a pledge today to place this cheque into an account in a bank, together with the proceeds from the sale of these properties, for the benefit of the families of all the victims who suffered at the hands of Bill Grady. I am asking Attorney Tom Saunders to deal with this on my behalf."

Steven then returned the letter and the contents to Tom Saunders.
All present praised Steven for his noble gesture.

When Steven, Raynor, and Janet returned home, Miranda greeted them and said that she had a surprise for them in the living room. It was Janet's sister, Mandy. She was an older version of Janet and gorgeous. She was a nurse. Steven and Mandy were meeting for the first time, and they were both delighted to meet each other. Was it love at first sight?

In December of that year, a beautiful baby girl was born to Janet and Raynor. They named her Ophelia.

One year later, Steven and Mandy were married.

ABOUT THE TRILOGY

After I wrote 'Zeeka Returns,' I compiled the first three books into one book. The book, received a five-star review from Readers Favorite International in September 2016.

Reviewed by Faridah Nassozi for Readers' Favorite-Five Stars.

In **Revenge of Zeeka: Horror Trilogy** by Brenda Mohammed, the island of Gosh is under attack by an army of zombies under the command of a vengeful science genius. In the year 2016, the Zika virus broke out in Central and South America with life-threatening effects for pregnant women. Given a choice to save the mothers or the unborn babies, a decision was made to save the mothers.

The tiny stillborns were securely and secretly buried. Only a few people knew of this. Unknown to everyone, however, a certain scientist managed to get hold of all 51 bodies, bring them back to life, and condition them to follow his command, creating himself a perfect army of zombies.

Now, twenty years later, the evil scientist seeks revenge on those he holds responsible for the stillbirths. Only three of the current doctors at Central Hospital, Raynor, Mark, and George, witnessed the unfortunate events of 2016.

The three have strong suspicions about who might be controlling the zombies. Meanwhile, Zeeka is lying in wait for the perfect time to unleash his army onto the island. Zeeka has big, evil plans and this is just the beginning. In a desperate search for answers, and with very little to go on, the doctors search for the elusive Master Zeeka.

Will they save the islanders from Zeeka and his zombies, or will it be too late? Revenge of Zeeka, by Brenda Mohammed, is a one-of-a-kind novella trilogy that delivers an incredible story guaranteed to give readers an absolute sci-fi treat.

I especially liked how Brenda used current events as the pivotal point from which to build this amazing sci-fi horror. This made the story even more relatable.

More importantly, however, I admired how she owned her story and created this captivating version of events. She captured with amazing depth the setting, characters, plot, and emotions in such few words. If you are looking for a thrilling short read, this fast-paced, sci-fi action novella will give you the time of your life."

ABOUT THE SERIES

In 2017, I added two more books to the series.

Zeeka's Ghost: Revenge of Zeeka Book 4.

Do you love ghost stories?
Then you would love Zeeka's Ghost.
The drama of the Zeeka Series continues in Zeeka's Ghost: Revenge of Zeeka Book 4.
This book is the fourth installment in the Medical fiction series, Zeeka Chronicles.
Swift. Silent. Ghostly, Zeeka's Ghost appears to Steven.

Does the ghost have evil intentions?
Are Steven and Mandy targets of unknown enemies?
Are their lives at stake?
Steven must find a way to hunt down and apprehend these ruthless maniacs and save his beloved wife.
Will he succeed?
Is Zeeka's Ghost here to harm or help?

Resurrection: Revenge of Zeeka Book 5.

Resurrection: Revenge of Zeeka Book 5 is the grand finale to the Science fiction series Zeeka Chronicles: Revenge of Zeeka.

Someone resurrected, and it is not Zeeka. Who is the stranger that Mandy's robot helper, Eve, encounters in the backyard? He claims to know Zeeka. Who is this stranger? When he learns that Eve is a robot, he tells her his story. Eve promises to keep their discussion a secret, but can she?

She records the conversation on her security device until she decides to play it for Steven and Mandy.

When the stranger collapses in the backyard with an epileptic fit, Eve alerts the Gosh hospital.

Tests and records reveal the stranger's identity.

Police records show that he died in the Carnival massacre in 2036, but did he?

Steven launches his greatest invention of the century.

Who will be the first volunteer to test it?

The identity of Number Nine is finally revealed. Get all the answers to your burning questions in the thrilling conclusion to the Zeeka series.

ZEEKA CHRONICLES

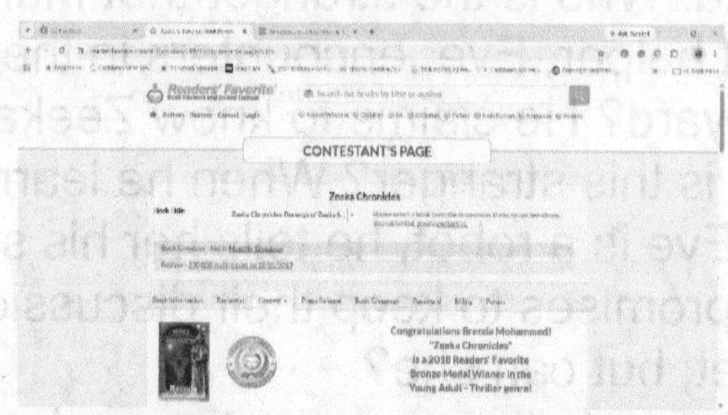

I also compiled all five books in the series into one book, **<u>Zeeka Chronicles: Revenge of Zeeka.</u>** The book received a five-star review and five-star seal from Readers' Favorite in February 2017, and won an award in the Readers' Favorite International Awards in 2018.

PRESS RELEASE FOR AWARD

For immediate release:

Readers' Favorite recognizes "Zeeka Chronicles" by Brenda Mohammed in its annual international book award contest.

The Readers' Favorite International Book Award Contest featured thousands of contestants from over a dozen countries, ranging from new independent authors to NYT best-sellers and celebrities.

Readers' Favorite is one of the largest book review and award contest sites on the Internet. They have earned the respect of renowned publishers like Random House, Simon & Schuster, and Harper Collins, and have received the "Best Websites for Authors" and "Honoring Excellence" awards from the Association of Independent Authors. They are also fully accredited by the BBB (A+ rating), which is a rarity among Book Review and Book Award Contest companies.

We receive thousands of entries from all over the world. Because of these large submission numbers, we are able to break down our contest into 140+ genres, and each genre is judged separately, ensuring that books only compete against books of their same genre for a fairer and more accurate competition. We receive submissions from independent authors, small publishers, and publishing giants such as Random House, HarperCollins and Simon & Schuster, with contestants that range from the first-time, self-published author to New York Times bestsellers like J.A. Jance, James Rollins, and #1 best-selling author Daniel Silva, as well as celebrity authors like Jim Carrey (Bruce Almighty), Henry Winkler (Happy Days), and Eriq La Salle (E.R., Coming to America).

"When the right books are picked as winners we pay attention. We will be spreading the word about Readers' Favorite." --Karen A., Editor for Penguin Random House

Readers' Favorite is proud to announce that "Zeeka Chronicles" by Brenda Mohammed won the Bronze Medal in the Young Adult - Thriller category.

You can learn more about Brenda Mohammed, "Zeeka Chronicles," read reviews, the author's biography, as well as connect with her directly through her website and social media pages.

Readers' Favorite LLC
Media Relations
Louisville, KY 40202

PRESS RELEASE FOR REVIEW

The author's new book receives a warm literary welcome. Readers' Favorite announces the review of the Science Fiction book "Zeeka Chronicles" by Brenda Mohammed.
Readers' Favorite is one of the largest book review and award contest sites on the Internet. They have earned the respect of renowned publishers like Random House, Simon & Schuster, and Harper Collins, and have received the "Best Websites for Authors" and "Honoring Excellence" awards from the Association of Independent Authors.

They are also fully accredited by the BBB (A+ rating), which is a rarity among Book Review and Book Award Contest companies.

"Reviewed By Sarah Stuart for Readers' Favorite.

Zeeka Chronicles: Revenge of Zeeka by Brenda Mohammed opens with Zeeka and the Zombies. On the island of Gosh in January 2036, Raynor Sharpe is woken by rattling to find a beach full of small robots. Is he still dreaming? Raynor is a hospital doctor and so is the woman he secretly loves, but Janet is engaged to another man.

Gosh's carnival is turned from an exotic native spectacle to tragedy by a troop of entertainers: zombies who shoot into the audience, killing and injuring hundreds. How can these monsters disintegrate into a heap of dust? Why is one false head found? Who is Zeeka, and does he control the zombies? Why does Janet cancel her wedding? Can the Chief of Police be trusted, or is he as corrupt as others in the force? Read on: Zeeka's Child, Zeeka Returns, Zeeka's

Ghost, and Resurrection hold the un-guessable answers.
Zeeka Chronicles comprises five books from the Revenge of Zeeka series in which 2036 is shown as a technically advanced world with gadgets like watches that seem like today's smartphones, plus visual contact, robots, and much more.
The story is built on the premise that a doctor discovers a cure for a disease but is prevented from using it.
However, the plot becomes more entangled the farther you read, with police corruption, suicide, kidnapping, and a very active ghost. Brenda Mohammed's writing style is evocative of the future, and she handles the science in her fiction brilliantly: reading is believing! I loved Zeeka Chronicles; it has worldwide appeal for anyone looking for an entertaining story that is different."
You can learn more about Brenda Mohammed, "Zeeka Chronicles," and the author's biography, as well as connect with the author directly or

through her website and social media pages.
Readers' Favorite LLC

AUTHOR 'S BIOGRAPHY

OVERVIEW

Brenda Mohammed is a prolific, multi-award-winning author and screenwriter from Trinidad and Tobago, with 68 published books and 68 audiobooks spanning various genres, including science fiction, memoirs, mystery, romance, self-help, poetry, children's books, anthologies, magazines, and three screenplays. Her superb writing skills won her several International literary awards, bringing fame to Trinidad and Tobago in the field of Literature. Brenda Mohammed's literary catalogue is a testament to the power of words, creativity, and resilience.

INTERNATIONAL RECOGNITION

1. Biz Weekly published Brenda's work in September 2025.
2. Her literary journey was published in USA NEWS in September 2025.
3. The Ethiopian Herald published an interview with Brenda Mohammed in 2021.
4. Her work in Literature was featured in the local newspapers in Trinidad and Tobago on several occasions.

PREVIOUS OCCUPATIONS

a. Before her literary ascent, Brenda was a trailblazer in banking and insurance, rising from a clerk at the tender age of 16 to senior leadership at a local bank in Trinidad. Her career helped shape communities and drive economic growth across Trinidad and Tobago.

b. After she retired from Banking, she excelled in insurance, earning the prestigious Million Dollar Round Table qualification six times, and a Life Underwriting Fellowship from the American College, USA, and earning international recognition as a top-tier financial professional from Trinidad and Tobago.

LITERARY JOURNEY AND ACCOLADES

1. Her writing journey began after surviving a near-fatal battle with cancer. That experience birthed I AM CANCER FREE, a bestselling memoir that won global acclaim. The book won an award in the Reader's Favorite International Awards 2018.

2. Her gripping five-series futuristic Caribbean sci-fi thriller, ZEEKA CHRONICLES, won an award in the Reader's Favorite International Awards 2018, and has been adapted into a five-part screenplay, primed for film or

television. The book also won awards in Science Fiction in SIBA Awards 2017, won the gold award in the category Science Fiction in Connections Emagazine Readers' Choice Awards 2018, and was in the top ten finalists for science fiction in the Author Academy Global Awards 2018.

3. Her four-series futuristic sci-fi horror screenplay, ZEEKA AND THE ZOMBIES II, is a finalist in a film and screenplay contest 2025, by 13Horror-com. This recognition marks a major milestone in Brenda's journey to bring her literary universe to the screen, reinforcing her reputation as a visionary storyteller with global impact

4. Her romance novel, THE GIFT OF LOVE, has also been adapted into a short screenplay for television and made it to the Quarterfinals of the Stage 32 DramaBox Screenwriting Competition in April 2026.

5. Her memoir, MY LIFE AS A BANKER, won second place for 'best memoir' in the Metamorph Publishing Summer Indie Book Awards 2016.

6. Her self-help guide, HOW TO WRITE FOR SUCCESS I, was hailed by the Ethiopian Herald as “a comprehensive toolkit for writers, critics, and editors.” In August 2019, How to Write for Success I topped all the books in the Non-Fiction category of Connections Emagazine Readers' Choice awards and won the gold medal in the non-fiction category. It also placed second in all categories and won the silver medal. It was a triple victory for Brenda, because her romance novel, 'Stories People Love,' placed first in all categories and won the gold medal.

7. BARRY HOLMES MYSTERIES received a five-star review from Readers' Favorite International in September 2021, won the Culture, Literature, and Research [CLR] Award in India for Best Writer- Fantasy, received a certificate of recognition from The International Chamber of Writers and Artists [CIESART], Spain in 2023 on World Book Day, and was a finalist in the Independent Author Awards 2024 hosted by Literary Global Awards.

8. STORIES PEOPLE LOVE topped the Connections Emagazine Readers' Choice Awards 2019, and won two gold medals in the category Romance and the other for topping all genres.
9. In 2025, CIESART GLOBAL honoured Brenda Mohammed with the UNION OF NATIONS SUCCESS AWARD and the MEDAL OF HONOUR for her outstanding career, significant merits, and valuable contributions in the fields of humanities, culture, science, and intercultural dialogue. Her picture was chosen as the face on CIESART'S GLOBAL MAGAZINES twice between 2023 and 2026.

LITERARY APPOINTMENTS

1. She was appointed by the President of CIESART GLOBAL as National President for CIESART [Cámara Internacional de Escritores & Artistas] Trinidad and Tobago, in 2022.
2. She founded the How to Write for Success Facebook Literary Forum in 2016 and has mentored countless writers, published anthologies, and

magazines that uplift voices worldwide. She continues to champion literature as a force for good. Her leadership has provided a space where writers are not only creators but crusaders, using their craft to heal, educate, and inspire.

3. A Peace Ambassador for the Facebook group, LOGOS LITERATURE, and advocate against domestic and all types of violence and suicide, Brenda's influence extends beyond the page.

4. She's a member of Stage 32, connecting her to the global film and TV community, and continues to inspire through humanitarian work, literary leadership, and cinematic storytelling.

In a world where stories shape lives, Brenda Mohammed emerges as a beacon, her words healing wounds, building communities, and transforming the literary landscape from Trinidad and Tobago to the world stage.

Her catalogue showcases not only her immense talent but also her deep commitment to addressing both personal and global challenges through storytelling.

Below is a curated overview of her diverse and impactful body of work.

CHILDREN'S BOOKS: NURTURING YOUNG MINDS AND HEARTS.

Brenda's children's books introduce young readers to the world through heart-warming stories that captivate the imagination while imparting valuable lessons.

Adventures of Squeaky Doo (2014) takes readers on the travel memoirs of a beloved teddy bear, sharing the wonder of discovery.

She Cried for Me (2017) offers a poignant autobiography from the perspective of a stray dog, combining empathy with an important message about compassion.

The Child Poet (2020) brings poetry to children, inviting them into a poetic galaxy full of wonder and creativity. This book became a hot release upon publication, delighting young minds with verse.

PSYCHOLOGICAL THRILLERS: UNRAVELLING MINDS AND MYSTERIES.

Brenda's psychological thrillers are gripping, fast-paced, and designed to keep readers on the edge of their seats. Her ability to weave suspense with character complexity makes her a standout in the genre.
The Manipulator (2021) delves deep into the mind of a manipulative figure, leaving readers questioning trust and human behaviour.
Conspiracy Stories (2021) features three chilling tales that awaken the mind and explore the dark side of human nature.

MYSTERY THRILLERS: TALES OF CRIME, SUSPENSE, AND ROMANCE

The Barry Holmes Series (2020), a mix of crime fiction and romance, is one of

Brenda's most popular works, capturing the intrigue and mystery of disappearances and unsolved crimes. Three mysterious disappearances bring together three mind-bending mysteries that leave readers questioning the truth. The Gift of Love (2018) mixes crime fiction with romance, engaging readers in a plot that keeps them guessing. The Axe Murderer (2019) takes on kidnapping and suspense, blending shocking twists with emotional depth. What Happened to Mary Loo (2020) explores the mystery of a post-lockdown disappearance.

.

MEMOIRS: SHARING STORIES OF LIFE AND RESILIENCE

Brenda's memoirs offer an intimate look at her life and the experiences that have shaped her. These stories of resilience, family, and career offer inspiration and reflection.

I Am Cancer Free (2013) recounts her miraculous recovery from cancer, offering hope and strength to others facing illness.

Memoirs of Dr. A. M. Khan (2014) sheds light on her father's life during Indentureship in Trinidad and Tobago, revealing a deeply personal family history.

My Life as a Banker (2014) chronicles Brenda's journey through the banking sector, offering motivational insights into the world of business.

Retirement is Fun (2014) captures the adventures and joys of life after her banking career, showcasing her ability to find fulfilment in new chapters.

Travel Memoirs with Pictures (2014) presents a visual journey around the world, blending storytelling with the beauty of photography.

CHRISTIAN BOOKS OF FAITH, INSPIRATION, AND WISDOM

Blending poetic inspiration with biblical teachings, Brenda's Christian books speak to the heart, providing spiritual guidance and encouragement.

Titles like Your Time Is Now, He is the One, Chosen by the Creator, God Fearing Ones, and Serenity in End Times (2014–2024) offer uplifting messages and biblical wisdom to help readers navigate life's challenges. True Power of Love and Now is the Time encourage faith-driven living, while Keys to Withstanding Storms of Life and Highway to Joy Eternal offer practical advice to find strength in times of hardship. Christmas Messages [2025] tells why Jesus is the reason for the season.

POETRY COLLECTIONS: REFLECTIONS OF THE SOUL.

Brenda's poetry collections have touched readers' hearts by addressing universal themes of love, resilience, and identity.
Collections like Strength for the Disheartened, Dreams of the Heart, and A Road Travelled (2019–2024) explore emotions ranging from loss to joy.

Chaotic Times (2021) captures the complexities of life, while Just for You and Treasured Memories celebrate love and personal reflection.

Sweet Medley [2020], Tea Time Poetry [2021] , Truth [2021], and Save God's Earth [2024] cover Climate Change, Environmental Issues, and Fun Times.

Soothing Poetry in English and Spanish [2020] covers several topics.

Beauty of poetry [2024] explores peace, love, motivation, and other emotions.

Islands in the Sun [2022] consists of poems about the Caribbean Islands.

ROMANCE: HEARTFELT AND ENDEARING TALES

Brenda's romance novels capture the beauty and complexity of relationships with heart-warming and tender narratives.

Stories People Love (2014) and Heart-Warming Tales (2014) explore themes of love, connection, and the magic of romance. Stories that Intrigue (2019) presents a unique love story between two writers, blending creativity and passion.

SCIENCE FICTION – REVENGE OF ZEEKA SERIES – A FUTURISTIC SAGA

Brenda's Zeeka Chronicles is a science fiction series that combines thrilling narratives with futuristic elements, such as zombies, robots, and human resilience, where good triumphs over evil.
Titles like Zeeka and the Zombies (2016), Zeeka's Child, Zeeka Returns, and Zeeka's Ghost (2017) create a post-apocalyptic world where survival and courage are paramount. Resurrection, Revenge of Zeeka Horror Trilogy, and the award-winning Zeeka Chronicles (2016–2017) complete the saga, which was also adapted into a five-part screenplay, reaching new heights in the world of sci-fi.
The Zeeka Chronicles is a remarkable contribution to the genre, mixing

imagination with powerful themes of survival and human spirit.
ZEEKA AND THE ZOMBIES II (2025) has earned the distinction of becoming a finalist in the 13Horror.com Screenplay Contest 2025, further solidifying its place as a ground-breaking work in both literature and visual media.

SELF-HELP & WRITING GUIDES: EMPOWERING THE NEXT GENERATION OF WRITERS.

Through her self-help books, Brenda shares invaluable knowledge and experience with aspiring authors.
How to Write for Success I, and II (2017, 2021) and Self-Publishing Tips (2022) provide practical advice for budding authors, helping them navigate the complexities of the writing and publishing world.

POETRY ANTHOLOGIES AND MAGAZINES: Amplifying Voices for Change

Brenda has also edited and co-authored poetry anthologies that address vital social issues.
A Spark of Hope I, II, and III (2019–2023) and Break the Silence I, II, and III (2020–2025) tackle topics such as suicide prevention, domestic violence, human trafficking, and addiction.
Peace Begins with Us (2022) and Creating a Better World (2022) encourage readers to take action for positive change.
CIESART Humming Bird Magazines I, II, III, and IV, and How to Write for Success, Magazines I, II, III, IV, and V contain news articles, poetry, and relevant issues for World Literature.
Check out her pages on her Website.

ZEEKA RETURNS: REVENGE OF ZEEKA

Published by Brenda Mohammed

www.ingramcontent.com/pod-product-compliance
Lightning Source LLC
LaVergne TN
LVHW031339150826
845673LV00012B/2967

* 9 7 8 1 5 2 0 6 6 0 4 8 6 *